MY FATHER'S RIVAL

A Silver Saints MC Novella

FIONA DAVENPORT

Copyright © 2017 by Fiona Davenport

Cover designed by Elle Christensen.

All rights reserved.

No part of this book may be reproduced in any form or by any electronic or mechanical means, including information storage and retrieval systems, without written permission from the author, except for the use of brief quotations in a book review.

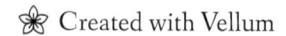

❦ Created with Vellum

Prologue

Bridget

NUDGING the kitchen door open with my foot, since I was holding two glasses of sweet tea in my hands, I stopped dead in my tracks and it almost smacked me straight in the face. When I'd arrived back at the compound, one of the prospects told me that I'd have to wait to talk to my dad because he was busy. I wasn't surprised since I was used to playing second fiddle to club business. It wasn't that my dad didn't love me—he absolutely did—but he had a lot of responsibilities on his shoulders as president of the Hounds of Hellfire MC.

Instead of complaining, I decided to make a

batch of my dad's favorite drink—besides whiskey or beer. I was hoping it would soften him up a little for whatever he'd called me to the clubhouse to talk about. Only I was shocked that his meeting was with the last person I ever expected to see there.

Jared "Mac" MacKenzie.

President of the Silver Saints MC.

My father's rival.

And my secret crush ever since I first laid eyes on him a year ago.

He was twenty years older than me, but that didn't stop me from fantasizing about what it would be like to be with him. To run my fingers through his light brown hair. Feel those muscles under my hands. Trace his tattoos with my fingers. Maybe my tongue, too. To feel his beard scrape against my skin as he claimed my mouth. And to tilt my head back and stare into his pale green eyes and find them looking *at* me instead of *through* me like I wasn't even there.

He didn't notice me gawking at him as he stormed through the clubhouse, slamming the door on his way out. Had no idea I took several steps forward, following after him until I heard the roar of his motorcycle's engine. Would never know that I flinched when my dad called out my name because it pulled me out of my Mac stupor and brought me back to reality. The one where I knew I'd never have a chance with him.

"As if there was even a remote possibility of that ever happening," I mumbled to myself as I changed direction and headed to my dad's office. A man like Mac had no interest in a girl like me, no matter how much dreaming I did about him. And if he ever did, my dad would put a stop to it anyway. If I wasn't sure about it before, the thunderous look on his face when I found him sitting behind his desk would have convinced me that it was hopeless.

"Hey, Daddy. I made you some tea," I said softly as I held a glass out to him.

"Thanks, princess," he grumbled, taking the drink from me before he pointed at a chair. "Sit down. We need to talk."

I did as he asked, just like always, crossing my ankles and smoothing the knee-length skirt of my sundress over my legs after I got settled in my seat. "Is everything okay?"

"No. Not even close." My heart started to hammer in my chest at his response. My dad wasn't one to show weakness; not even with me. Seeing the scared look on my face, he heaved a deep sigh. "But it will be. Things are fucked up right now, but I'll figure a way out of it. I always do."

I couldn't imagine a situation that would get the best of him, so I was quick to agree. "I'm sure you will, Daddy."

"In the meantime, I need you to stick close to home more than usual. The boys will keep an eye on you, like they always do."

"I'm supposed to start my new job next week," I reminded him. A feeling of dread started to creep over my skin.

"It'll be easier on all of us if you're here or at the house instead of running around town. The job can wait."

"But–"

"I'm not asking you, Bridget. I'm telling you," he growled.

"I don't think they'll be able to hold the job for me if it's going to be more than a week. The library's already short-staffed, and I was lucky they were willing to give me a week off after graduation before I started." My hands twisted in my lap as I silently pleaded with him to understand. I really wanted this job.

His deep blue eyes, the exact same color as mine, held a hint of apology. But his face looked like it was carved from stone. "I know how much you were looking forward to working there, but your safety comes first. And I can't risk having you in town that much right now."

"Does this have something to do with the Silver Saints MC?"

"It's club business, princess." Which meant I wasn't going to get any more of an explanation about what was going on; not even if I lost my job over the situation. Whatever it was. "Stick close to home. Stay alert. And stay the fuck away from anyone in a Silver Saints cut. Especially Mac."

Chapter One

Mac

"FUCKING HOUNDS," I grunted as I used my fist to open the door to my office. It flew back and smashed into the wall, startling the tall, lanky man sitting behind my desk.

Kyle "Scout" West, my VP, took one look at my face and frowned fiercely. "He refused?"

I lifted my chin as I rounded the desk and he stood to vacate my spot. "Wouldn't fucking budge." Flopping down into my chair, I stifled the impulse to smash something else. "Barely acknowledged he even knew about the incident."

Three days ago, Logan, my Road Captain, ended

up in the hospital after a fight broke out at a local street race. Seemed he'd stepped in when another man got too rough with a woman, and the other man had brought a baseball bat into the brawl.

All we knew about the motherfucker was that he had been wearing a Hounds of Hellfire cut and Logan was in a fucking coma so he couldn't call out the bastard.

I wanted retribution—to teach the fucker how to treat a woman and to never mess with a Silver Saint unless they wanted the wrath of the entire MC to rain down on them. But the only way to figure out the identity of the club member was through their Prez. None of his members would betray the brotherhood.

Everyone knew that Pierce's only weakness was his pampered little princess of a daughter. I'd made the mistake of assuming the jackass would be outraged that one of his men would mistreat a woman.

"What next?" Scout asked. The rigid angles of his face were made harsher by a deep scowl and his gray eyes were screaming for blood. As if his appearance wasn't intimidating enough, he'd been a scout sniper in the marines and just about everyone except me was at least a little afraid of him.

I had held on to a plan as a last resort, and I didn't see any other choice. "We take something from him to bargain with."

Scout's mouth quirked up at the corner, but it was a menacing smirk. "Which of his sorry ass brothers do I get to put the screws to?"

I shook my head and opened the laptop perched on the desktop. "They aren't good enough. Has to be someone he would give anything to get back." My fingers typed quickly until I found what I was looking for. A local newspaper article about a book drive put on at the library in town. Flipping the computer around, I pointed to the screen where a small group was smiling for the camera. A willowy, red head stood at the edge, her smile bright but shy. "Bridget Pierce."

"You want to go after his kid?" Scout asked, his tone incredulous. "You have a fucking death wish, Mac?"

"She's the only one with the amount of leverage we need."

"Might be right about that," he admitted gruffly. "But how the fuck are we supposed to get our hands on her? He keeps her locked up tight in her little castle or surrounded with his boys. And unless he's lost his damn mind, he'll have her under extra security after your meeting today."

I leaned back in my chair and rubbed a hand over my beard, thinking. "Their next run. May have beefed up her security, but that will leave the compound a little thin." I grinned mockingly at Scout. "I'm thinking your skills have gotten a little rusty. A mission like this is just what you need." He'd use tranqs to clear me a path and he'd do it at night, from as far as one thousand yards away.

"Fuck you," he snapped even as he returned my grin. "I'm a fucking God with a rifle"—his smile turned lewd—"and any other *weapon*. Just ask Cat."

I rolled my eyes and flipped him the bird. Cat was Scout's old lady and I had zero desire to talk to her about his prowess beyond a sniper rifle. "Get your ass outta my office."

WE PARKED our hogs a mile away and loaded into a black van driven by one of our prospects. He dropped us near the back of the compound and then nestled the vehicle near the edge of the surrounding woods.

It only took about ten minutes before we spotted

two members patrolling the electric fence surrounding their property. One at a time, they fell to the ground as Scout's silent ammunition struck them.

"Probably got ten minutes before they send someone out to check on those two," Hack, an enforcer, informed me through my ear bud. "After Scout takes them down, maybe another five before they sound the alarm."

I grunted a reply and crept up to the fence. Trading my riding gloves for thick, complete leather ones, I nodded to the brother with me, Grub. He handed me a pair of razor sharp, plastic wire cutters.

Reputation and appearance went a long way in protecting the Hounds compound, and I knew they kept the electric charge at a lower voltage because they felt secure in the other aspects. Still, without the proper precaution, touching the crisscross metal would knock me on my ass and keep me shuddering for a while.

With that in mind, I carefully cut a large arch into the fence, then pulled it open and secured it with rubber clips. I tossed my tools back to Grub and once again changed out my gloves. I went with thin, black leather this time. It gave me more dexterity since I didn't need protection from the electricity at this point.

"Going in," I murmured.

"Three minutes down," Hack grumbled. "Move your ass and don't get caught."

I didn't take the time to respond with a scathing comment, instead focusing on slipping through the hole I'd made. The president of an MC usually lived at the clubhouse, unless he's got a family. Pierce was paranoid and didn't want to be far, but he didn't want his precious daughter living in the clubhouse. So, he'd built a private addition off the back.

Other than guards and a few prospects, most of the club was helping with their current run because it was one of their biggest clients. He hadn't skimped on the protection though, and I knew I'd have to deal with one or two guys if I tried to get inside on the main floor.

A few days of recon had shown us which windows Bridget seemed to pass by the most and we'd determined that her bedroom was at the top right, the one with a balcony. At well over six feet, it only took me a running leap to grab hold of the bottom and pull myself up enough to shift my grip to the railing. Spending hours at the gym and in the ring definitely paid off.

I shook my head in exasperation when I realized the sliding glass door was unlocked. The kid was clueless. Silently, I slid it open and stepped into the moonlit room. I scanned the space until my eyes landed on the bed, then shuffled over until I stood at the side.

Fuck me running.

The girl lying on the bed had thrown off the covers and was dressed in only a thin tank top and tiny shorts. This was no kid though. She was a woman, from her gorgeous red hair splayed on her pillow, to her plump, kiss-me lips, to her generous tits, to her long—fucking long legs. My cock swelled, and my mouth watered.

I was in deep fucking shit.

Chapter Two

Bridget

I'D BEEN FEELING RESTLESS EVER since I'd had that talk with my dad. Or maybe it was from seeing Mac in the clubhouse. Either way, I'd barely been able to eat or sleep, and it hadn't gotten any better tonight. If anything, it was worse since I'd had the hardest time falling asleep. I'd tossed and turned, waking up three times already. I was cold, jumpy, and irritable.

"Not again," I mumbled under my breath, reaching for my sheet and blanket. My hope was that I'd be able to fall back asleep if I could get warm again. Then I caught a glimpse of something out of the corner of my eye, and I figured I must be having one of those dreams where you thought you were awake but you really weren't. Because that some*thing* I'd caught sight of was actually a some*one*. And not just anyone. It was...

"Mac," I breathed out before it registered that what I was seeing was not a dream. As he stalked towards me, quickly closing the space between my bed and the sliding glass doors leading to the balcony, I realized he was actually in my room. For real. Dressed all in black; leather jacket under his cut, shirt, jeans, boots, and gloves.

Jerking upright, I gasped, "What in the world?"

"Fuck," he gritted out. Those pale green eyes of his narrowed, raking up and down my body. Then his nostrils flared, and his lips firmed into a line. All of his focus was on me, just like I'd always wanted. Only I couldn't wrap my brain around it.

"You shouldn't be here," I hissed when he made it to the side of my bed. My gaze darted from him to the door and back again. My dad wasn't around, but I knew that he'd left guys to watch over the place because I was home. "Someone's going to catch you and then—"

He reached down to wrap his hand around my

arm, and I lost track of what I'd been trying to say. "Quiet," he ordered.

"But—"

"If you can't keep quiet, you'll be right—someone will figure out I'm here. But you'll also be wrong because they're not gonna catch me. They try to get in my way, what they're gonna get is hurt. Doesn't matter how many men I have to go through; you're coming with me."

"Coming with you?" I echoed. I shook my head in confusion, and his fingers tightened on my arm.

He bent down low, his face only inches from mine. "You heard me. We can do this the easy way or the hard way. Choice is yours." His gaze dropped down to my chest, where my pebbled nipples were poking against my tank. "If you're looking for an incentive to go the easy route, cooperation means I don't have to carry your ass outta here dressed like you are right now." His expression darkened, the idea really seeming to piss him off.

Considering I only ever wore this little clothing in the privacy of my bedroom—and that the man doing the talking was Mac—the decision was simple. "I have a sweater and jeans I can toss over my pajamas."

He lifted a hand, and one long finger traced the

strap of my tank on my shoulder. I felt the heat rise in my cheeks, a mixture of shyness and desire evoked by being so close to my fantasy man with barely any clothes on. "Get 'em on. Now."

When he stepped back and jerked his head towards my closet, I scurried off my mattress. It only took me a minute to grab what I needed and toss it on. Then I shoved a pair of socks onto my feet and slid on a pair of gym shoes. As soon as I was done, Mac led me out the sliding glass door and onto my balcony.

"Shit!" he grunted.

"What's wrong?" I whispered. I squinted my eyes and tried to peer around, worried that he'd spotted one of the guys and something awful was about to happen.

"Just trying to figure out how the hell I'm gonna get you down safely."

I glanced over the railing at the ground, surprised that I didn't see a ladder. "How'd you get up here?"

"Jumped and pulled myself up," he muttered distractedly. Like it was no big deal, and it didn't make him sexier than he already was. "If I drop down first, I can catch you but you'll have to be careful going over the railing. Or,"—his eyes raked up and down my body again—"I can lower you down far enough that you'll be able to fall the rest of the way without getting hurt. You're light enough that it'll work."

I jerked my finger to the left. "Or we could just use the fire escape ladder my dad got me for that window. He kind of goes overboard when it comes to my safety."

"Not nearly fucking enough," he grumbled as he followed me back into my room and over to the window. When I bent over to pick up the ladder, he nudged me out of the way. I had to bite my lip to stifle a nervous giggle at the ridiculousness of him being pissed at my dad for me not being more protected when he was in the middle of kidnapping me. I'd barely managed to contain myself by the time he had the ladder set up and glowered at me. "You're gonna go down first. And don't forget to be quiet, or else my man out there is going to have to take out anyone who comes to investigate what's going on."

I gulped a little at the reminder of how serious this situation was and nodded my head. I carefully climbed out the window, hooked my feet into the rungs beneath me, and almost lost my footing when I found myself chest to face with Mac. My sweater did a better job of covering my nipples than my tank had, but they were still visibly poking against the material. Mac's gaze was zeroed in on them, making my breasts feel heavier as my nipples grew even harder.

"Move," he ordered.

I scurried down the ladder and quietly waited for him to follow when I reached the ground. It didn't take long, and then we were racing towards the fence—his hand wrapped around mine as I tried to keep up with his long strides. I stumbled when I saw two bodies on the ground, about fifteen feet down the fence line from us. Mac turned to steady me, noticed where my eyes were glued, and lifted me into his arms.

"They're not dead; only knocked out," he rasped in my ear. "Although they deserve a fuck of a lot more than the headaches they'll wake up with for being so goddamn lax on the job when they were supposed to protect you. Sneaking in to grab the princess of the Hounds of Hellfire should have been a lot harder than it was."

I didn't have time to consider why he'd be so angry at my dad's men when they'd made his job easier; not with him practically dragging me to a black van parked near the woods behind the compound. The engine was running, and the back doors were open. Mac shoved me inside, closing the doors behind us after he climbed in.

I swallowed my yelp when I saw there were three men waiting for us; the driver, a guy in the passenger seat, and one in the back who caught me before I fell on the floor. Mac yanked me out of his arms and held onto me as the van wrenched forward. We all sat in silence for the couple of minutes we drove down the street. When we stopped, the doors swung open and a tall guy with a VP patch on his cut peered inside. His gray eyes locked on me. "Did I see what I thought I saw? She provided the ladder for her own kidnapping?"

Yup. That was me. The girl who helped the guy of her dreams—her dad's rival, the one he'd warned her to stay away from—smuggle her out of her bedroom in the middle of the night. I was either the smartest girl ever...or the dumbest.

Chapter Three

M^{ac}

DAMN, she felt good in my arms. Too fucking good. I quickly shoved her at Scout, frustrated at my reaction to her. "She rides with you." His eyebrows shot up to his hairline, but I ignored him as I hopped out of the van. I kept my eyes averted, so I wouldn't see how she responded to my order. If she liked the idea of being near Scout, I was afraid I'd rip his fucking head off. However, I couldn't help watching her hips and tight ass sway as she walked away from me.

I stalked to my hog and got on, slamming my foot down on the kick starter. Scout's engine revved and I looked jerkily in his direction. Bridget was sitting on the back of his bike, her slim arms wrapped around Scout's torso. Even though Scout already had an old lady, something inside me howled in protest at the sight of her clinging to him. To anyone but me. It didn't seem to matter that she was too fucking young for me. Too sweet and innocent.

"Fuck," I muttered before yelling to be heard over the noise from the bikes, "Bridget! Get over here."

Scout's head pivoted, and he smirked at me before helping her off the seat. I scowled darkly, my eyes threatening retribution if he said even one fucking word. Bridget hesitated when she caught sight of my expression. I held out my hand and beckoned her forward with my fingers, softening my look so she wouldn't be afraid.

I handed her a helmet and fastened the straps, tucking her red hair out of her face. "Hop on, baby," I growled. "We need to get the fuck outta here."

She climbed on and wrapped her arms around me tightly. Her tits pressed flush against my back, and I could feel her heart racing. I rarely let any woman ride with me but when I had, it had never felt this good. She fit me like a glove. Shaking my head, I tried to dispel the thoughts invading my mind and took off like a bat outta hell.

We reached the Silver Saints compound a little less than an hour later. Once inside the main garage, I shut off my bike and helped Bridget to her feet. As she swung her leg over, she lost her balance and went tumbling into my chest.

Son of a bitch. Riding with her wrapped around me had made me hard as fuck but when she was pressed against my front, I thought my dick was gonna burst through my damn jeans. She looked up at me with wide, deep blue eyes, her pink lips slightly parted, and her skin flushed. I could too easily imagine how she would look after being thoroughly fucked and I shoved her away quickly, trying to get some control.

I hadn't kidnapped her to make her my plaything. I didn't roll that way—she was simply leverage for the swap. I had no intention of corrupting Pierce's innocent little princess, no matter how tempting the idea was. The last thing I needed was to jeopardize the plan by getting involved with her. *Besides*, I reminded myself, *she's too damn young for you.* I was old enough to be her motherfucking father.

After removing her helmet, I grasped her arm and towed her behind me to the clubhouse. "Do what I tell you, keep out of the way, and you'll be headed home to your palace as soon as your asshole father does what I want," I explained as we walked.

We entered through a side door so I could take her down the hall to my office without parading her through the front room. Just the idea of anyone else leering at her had my blood boiling. I was so intent on our destination that I almost plowed into Cat when she stepped out of the kitchen.

Cat looked Bridget up and down before turning to me with a curious and slightly disgusted expression. "That Pierce's little princess?" she asked.

"Bridget," I corrected, surprisingly irritated at Cat's description and attitude. "Don't want any of the other girls or old ladies hassling her." I gave Cat a hard look. "I'm putting you in charge of her."

Cat narrowed her grassy green eyes and pursed her lips for a moment, but simply nodded.

"Making the call to Pierce now, then I'll put her in my room."

Cat's eyebrows practically went through the roof, and Bridget made a muffled noise that I didn't take the time to interpret. Cat clearly thought I'd lost my mind, and I didn't completely disagree with her. Yeah, it was a stupid fucking move but while I would trust my brothers with my life, I didn't trust them with Bridget.

I stepped around Cat, effectively dismissing her, and continued dragging Bridget to my office. Inside, I slammed the door shut and walked her to a worn couch pushed up against the left wall. "Sit." When she obeyed without question, I nodded and went to sit at my desk.

My eyes strayed to Bridget as I dialed Pierce's number. She was gazing around the room, her eyes more curious than apprehensive. Her reactions to everything were throwing me off kilter. I'd expected her to be terrified and to throw a spoiled tantrum, not to be so damn cooperative.

"Whaddyou want, Mac?" Pierce grunted when he answered.

"Same thing I wanted the last time we talked, jackass," I snarled.

"Well fuck off. Haven't changed my mind and I'm not gonna."

"How about a trade?"

"Ain't nothin' you got that I'd ever want, Mac."

"That's where you're wrong, Pierce," I sneered smugly. I put the phone on speaker and pointed at Bridget. "Say hello to Daddy, princess."

She blanched and stared at me as she answered. "Um, hi Daddy."

"WHAT THE FUCK?" Pierce roared. Bridget

flinched, but I just smiled maniacally. "I will fucking kill you, Mac."

"Relax, Pierce. I have no intention of hurting or violating your perfect spawn. I'm suggesting a straight up trade. Bridget for the motherfucker who put my guy in a coma."

Pierce didn't say anything at first, the only sound his heavy breathing, as he tried to calm his temper. "It'll take me some time to find him—"

"One week," I snapped without letting him finish. "You don't have him by then, your little girl will have to earn her keep around here." I hung up before Pierce could get in another word.

Bridget's eyes were wide as she stared at me. Again, I was a little baffled by the small spark of curiosity shining through her alarm. I frowned as I stood and prowled over to stand in front of her. "No one will touch you," I assured her. "But, that doesn't mean I won't put you to work. This isn't your castle on a cloud, baby. You'll have to learn to dirty those hands."

Her beautiful blue eyes narrowed and she opened her mouth to speak but a knock on my door drew both our attentions.

"Yeah?"

Hack popped his head in and glanced at Bridget

before his eyes landed on me. "Club business, Prez."

I nodded and gestured for Bridget to stand. "Give me ten, and we'll meet back here."

"Sure thing." He left the door open when he spun around and disappeared down the hall.

"Follow me. Stay close and keep your head down," I instructed Bridget. I led her to a set of stairs and up, then down another hall to the door at the end. Opening the door, I lifted my chin, indicating that she should enter.

Her soft body brushed against mine as she walked over the threshold and I stifled a groan. I needed some damn air.

"Don't leave this room without me or Cat. Things are different when you don't have Daddy's protection. You walk around here without a cut, boys will think you're fair game. Understood?"

She nodded as she stood uncomfortably awkward in the center of the room, looking around. It wasn't as simple as the other rooms. I lived at the clubhouse permanently, and being the president had its perks. One being the king size bed that I was studiously ignoring for the moment. I showed her the bathroom and how to work the tv, then beat a hasty retreat before I did something truly stupid. Like kiss the fuck out of her plush, pink lips.

IT TOOK a couple of hours to straighten out the mess a couple of prospects had made on a run. Which meant it was almost three in the morning before I made my way back upstairs. Opening the door quietly, I listened to see if there was any indication that Bridget was awake. The room was dark, but in the glow of the moonlight, I was once again staring at the sexiest woman I'd ever seen. Except this time, she was curled up in *my* bed, like an offering from the devil himself. I knew I should turn right around and sleep on the couch in my office. But, my feet had their own agenda and made their way to the side of the bed. I sucked in a deep breath and by the time I'd exhaled it, I'd given in to temptation. I stripped to my boxers and slipped under the covers, fully intending to stay on my side.

Then Bridget sighed and rolled towards me. My determination not to touch her shattered, and I pulled her into my arms.

I didn't know what the fuck had come over me, but I was starting to suspect that she would be a lot harder to let go than I'd thought. And, one word was pulsing in my head with each beat of my heart.

Mine.

Chapter Four

Bridget

RAYS OF MORNING light shining through the blinds woke me. When I rolled over to stretch, I bumped up against a hard, warm body and yelped. My eyes popped open and all that had happened the night before came roaring back into my brain. Only one thing was missing from my memory...when had Mac climbed into bed with me? I wanted to kick myself for falling so sound asleep that I didn't even notice. It was just my luck that my restlessness ended the minute I was tucked in to his bed instead of mine, and I ended up missing out on the first interesting thing that could have woken me up. But at least I could enjoy the view now since he was still asleep.

"Oh, wow," I breathed out when he rolled towards me and the sheet shifted lower. He flung his arm over his face, covering his eyes. His glorious body, from the waist up, was on show. Inked skin stretched taut over muscles. A happy trail led under a sheet that was tented. *Holy moly.* The morning wood thing was apparently true, and Mac was packing what looked like a tree trunk in his pants.

I scooted down the mattress a little, and tugged at the sheet. When it got stuck on his hard on, I peeked up at his face to make sure he was still sleeping before lifting it off him so I could get a better look. His eyes were closed, and his chest continued to rise and fall in a steady rhythm. I breathed a soft sigh of relief since I had no desire to get caught, but then I almost groaned in disappointment when my gaze drifted lower only to find my view blocked by a pair of black boxers.

"Stop looking at me like that, baby. Before I do something we'll both regret," he rasped out, startling me. Heat swept up my neck as my head jerked up. His pale green eyes were heavy-lidded and focused on my face.

"But what if I wouldn't regret it?" Heat burned my cheeks as I asked the bold question.

He wrapped his fingers around my wrist, dragging me up and onto his chest. "Trust me. You would. You're just too damn young to know any better."

"Yeah, I'm young," I conceded. "But I'm not stupid."

He blew out a harsh breath and rubbed a hand over his face. "What you are is untouched, and I don't fuck virgins."

I tried to jerk away from him, but he didn't loosen his grip. "If you're not planning to touch me—to violate my dad's demon spawn—why am I in your bed? Why are you holding me tight instead of pushing me away?"

His hand drifted down my back to cup my butt. "You got it wrong, baby. I called you *perfect*, not a demon. And that's why you're here with me. Because you're too damn tempting." He drove his hips upwards and ground his hardness against me. "I ache with need for you. Never knew it could hurt this bad. But I'm not gonna take you."

"But why?" It didn't make any sense to me. Mac was the kind of guy who took what he wanted, and it certainly sounded like he wanted me. "Why not give in when we're both hurting?"

His eyes flared, and he cursed under his breath as he rolled me onto my back. Levering his body over mine, he lowered his head and captured my mouth. My body melted against his, and my lips parted when his tongue swept across them. My acceptance of his kiss earned me a guttural groan, and his hand dove into my hair. He tilted my head back as he devoured me—his tongue stroking deep inside my mouth, claiming me.

Then he parted my legs, settled his hips between them, and I whimpered against his lips. Every inch of our bodies were plastered together. His hard length was pressed against my opening, with only my sleep shorts and his boxers separating us. I was dizzy with need, my shorts quickly moving past damp to drenched.

"One fucking kiss," he rasped. "And you're almost ready to fly apart for me, aren't you?"

"Yes," I hissed, wiggling my hips. I wanted him closer. "Need more."

"So damn sweet." He wedged his face against my neck, nipping at the sensitive skin there. "There's no reason for us both to suffer, not when I can give you the relief that you need."

I shifted beneath him, and he groaned. His sensual promise made my core clench. My thighs tightened around him, and he gave a quick thrust of his hips that stroked his hard length up the center of my sleep shorts. "Mac," I gasped.

His teeth sank into the side of my neck, hard enough to leave a mark, and then he sat up between my legs with a hand holding my knees open. His eyes swept down my body, until they focused between my legs. "Look at that. I can see how turned on you are, right through those tiny shorts of yours." He flashed me a cocky grin. "Remind me to throw 'em the fuck away. Need to get you something else to wear to bed because you're too damn tempting in those. I'd lose my fucking shit if anyone else saw you dressed like this."

The possessive statement threw me for a loop since it was the last thing I expected to hear from him. I was the girl he'd kidnapped to seal a deal with my dad; not someone he should be jealous about. But I wasn't going to argue with him over it; not when it only made me want him more than I already did.

"Be a good girl and stay still for me," he ordered, tugging my shorts down my legs as he shuffled back to lie down at the end of the mattress. The new position put him right between my legs, his face in front of my bare pussy.

I squeezed my legs shut, as far as they would go with his body wedging them open, and shoved my hands down to cover myself. "Mac!"

His eyes were filled with a naughty gleam when he looked up at my face. "C'mon, princess. Open your legs and give me a taste of what I'm guessing is the sweetest pussy I'll ever get my mouth on."

The warmth of his breath against my hands made me shiver. Almost of their own volition, my legs fell open. I slowly lifted my hands, and my reward was a brush of his lips against the inside of my thighs. First one, then the other—leaving me quivering in anticipation. My focus was wholly on the feel of his warm lips against my skin, and the rough slide of his beard following after the wet trail he made up my legs. His hands were wrapped around the underside of my thighs, and his hold tightened when he leaned forward to trace up my center with his tongue.

I'd never felt anything like it. My entire body was stretched taut, warmth building in my lower belly as his mouth worked me. He built it, higher and higher. Long licks. Swirls around my clit. Nibbles along the lips of my sex. With his mouth open wide and tongue stroking, the pressure inside me reached a peak. I exploded, shouting his name. "Jared!"

He didn't pull back until I collapsed against the mattress, panting. "Haven't had anyone use my real name in longer than I can remember, but fuck if I don't want to hear you say it the same damn way over and over again as I make you come."

"I'm not going to argue. I really enjoyed that." That infernal blush heated my face once more. I couldn't believe the things that popped out of my mouth around him.

"Could tell," he grunted, lifting up to hover over my body. "You wanna do it again, all you have to do is ask. I'll eat you out as often as you like."

"As often as I'd like, huh? But don't you have an MC to run?"

"Fuck!" he shouted, punching the mattress. His face closed down, and I wished I could take the words back. I'd meant them to be a joke, but they only served as a reminder to him of all the reasons why he shouldn't touch me. As he pushed off the bed and stalked into the bathroom, a lone tear tracked down my cheek.

Chapter Five

Mac

"WHAT THE FUCK were you thinking, asshole?" I growled at myself in the bathroom mirror. I licked my lips and groaned at the taste of Bridget still lingering there.

I needed to stay the hell away from her. The last thing we needed was to be at war with the Hounds of Hellfire. My club wasn't exactly filled with boy scouts but Pierce's guys played dirty. Taking her as leverage was dangerous enough—there would be no coming back from fucking her while she was here.

The solution was to keep Bridget busy and out of my sight. I didn't have any other choice but to hand her over to Cat to find her something to do. I knew I should also find her another place to sleep but it would only distract me even more, worrying about her safety and obsessing over whose bed she was lying in. I'd simply have to make use of the couch in my office. There were plenty of beds that would welcome me, but I hadn't been interested in meaningless companionship for a long time and after getting a feel and taste of Bridget...she was the only one I craved.

I took a fortifying breath and opened the bathroom door. Bridget was still sitting on the bed in her tiny tank top, but she'd put back on her shorts. She looked up at me with confusion and desire in her eyes, and it almost broke my resolve. She was fucking gorgeous, and so tempting.

I shook my head to try and clear it as I stalked over to a worn, wooden dresser by the door. I grabbed a fresh pair of boxers, jeans, and a T-shirt. Then I snatched my cut from where it hung on the wall and tossed it onto the bed.

"I'll send someone with some fresh clothes for you," I told her gruffly. "You need to wear that when you leave this room. No one will bother you as long as you wear my brand." I made my way to the bathroom without waiting for her response, but paused in the doorway and looked at her. "What happened before"—I ran a frustrated hand through my hair—"that shit shouldn't have happened. You may have been raised in this life, princess, but you aren't cut out for it. I'm too fucking old to be making mistakes like getting involved with someone so young."

Her blue eyes deepened as hurt filled them, but they also held a stubborn glint that made me smile as I shut the bathroom door. After sending a quick text to Cat to rustle up some clothes for Bridget, I hopped in the shower and dressed for the day.

Our MC had its finger in a lot of businesses, but one of our main sources of income was a shop that specialized in racing bikes. We had a new shipment coming in, and that meant a shit ton of stuff to do.

When I exited the bathroom, Bridget was standing by the solitary window in the room, holding a bundle of clothes and shifting restlessly on her feet.

"Get ready, then meet me in my office," I ordered. I headed for the door and noticed my vest still on the unmade bed. "And don't forget the cut." Stepping into the hall, I blew out a heavy breath as I closed the door behind me. My room was filled with her delicious scent, and I practically ran away from it like a cowardly bitch.

Scout was waiting for me in my office, and I

scowled at the knowing grin on his face. "Cat said she delivered clothes to the little princess in your room this morning."

"And?" I growled.

He shrugged. "Noticed your couch looks untouched. I'm guessing that can't be said for our captive anymore."

"Keep your opinions to yourself and your mouth shut, brother." I dropped onto the seat behind my desk. "There a reason you're in my office? Or you just here to get your ass thrown out?" He toned down his grin to a slight smirk, but I still wanted to wipe it off his face with my fist.

"Delivery is confirmed for this afternoon. Got the boys lined up for the run tomorrow too. You still planning on going?"

It was the perfect excuse to get away from Bridget. By the time I got back, Pierce's time would be up.

"No." My hand balled into a fist as I mentally put a fucking gun to my head. "I need to be here in case Pierce comes through early." It was a pitiful attempt to excuse my answer, but Scout didn't question it. I was the fucking president and didn't need to explain myself.

We went over the details for the run and were

just finishing up when a soft knock on my door interrupted our conversation. "Yeah," I snapped.

Bridget opened the door and slowly walked inside. When she saw Scout, she straightened her spine and gave him a nod of greeting before walking to a chair in front of my desk and taking a seat. She'd donned my cut and something inside me calmed at the sight.

"Princess," he greeted her with a smirk.

She stiffened further and shocked me when she practically growled, "My name is Bridget."

Scout grinned and plopped down onto the chair beside her. "How about I call you, Blue, because of those gorgeous blue eyes?"

She cocked her head to the side and studied him for a moment, then gave him a small smile in return. "Blue it is."

I didn't like the idea of him having a special nickname for her, but calling him out on it would only show my developing weakness for her.

"Scout."

"Yeah, Prez?"

"Get out." My tone left no room for argument.

He stood and meandered to the open door. Cat appeared, and he winked at her. "Kitty Cat," he growled, and he smacked her ass before continuing down the hall. Her lips tipped up into a smile until she faced the room and noticed Bridget.

"Mac. What can I do for you?"

"I'm putting you in charge of Bridget," I explained. "Show her around, make sure she knows the places that are off limits, and find her something to do while she's here."

"You want me to babysit the pampered princess?" she asked in surprise and disgust. Bridget let out a cute little growl at the nickname and I suppressed a smile.

"You questioning my orders, woman?" I stared hard at her, leaving her without a doubt that I was serious and expected her to do what she was told.

She threw another glance at Bridget, revulsion clear in her eyes, then sighed and looked back at me. "No." She stood and motioned for Bridget to follow her. "Let's go, kid."

Bridget looked as though she wanted to say something to me, but changed her mind and quietly trailed after Cat.

I tried to get my mind back on work, though it frequently strayed to my blue-eyed beauty. Couldn't help wondering what she was doing and how she was adjusting. Then I'd lecture myself for being a pansy ass and throw myself back into my responsibilities.

When my stomach growled, I grabbed food from the kitchen and took it back to my office. Finally, my eyes grew tired and I glanced at the clock on my desk to see that it was after two in the morning. I trudged over to my couch and flopped down on it, determined to catch some shut eye and stay away from the woman currently occupying my bed. Instead, I tossed and turned until I finally gave up and went upstairs. I silently undressed and slipped into bed, pulling Bridget into my arms.

I woke with the sunrise and left before she knew I'd been there. It would have to be enough—sleeping with her in my arms.

Chapter Six
―――――――――

Bridget

WAKING up the second morning after Mac took me wasn't nearly as pleasurable as the first. Cat had kept me busy all day, and I'd been exhausted when she'd finally released me from being her slave-laborer after dinner clean-up. I'd tried to stay awake so I could talk to him, in the hope that I'd be able to convince him to let me spend my time with someone—anyone—other than Cat. Preferably him. But I must have passed out before he'd turned in for the night, and slept through him leaving since the bed was now empty. I would have thought I'd spent the entire night alone if it wasn't for the indentation on the pillow next to me and the slight hint of his scent on the sheets.

"I better see that man more today than I did yesterday," I mumbled to myself. "Or else I'll have to kick my own butt for cooperating in my own kidnapping."

My muscles ached when I crawled out of bed and headed into the bathroom to get ready for my day. Not that I needed to do a lot since I was just going to be a hot and sweaty mess soon because Cat clearly had it out for me. A fact that was proven to me yet again when I walked into the kitchen and she turned from the stove to glare at me.

"Did the spoiled princess get enough sleep? Would she like a cup of coffee? Maybe a gourmet breakfast?"

I didn't bother saying anything. I'd learned that lesson yesterday. Cat couldn't care less what I had to say or if she hurt my feelings. She'd made her mind up about me, and nothing was going to change it.

"Now that you're finally up, get over here and stir these eggs."

I did as she asked—or ordered, really, since it wasn't a request—and took her place at the stove. There were at least two dozen eggs in the pan, and Cat hurried over to the toaster to pull out four slices of toast. She popped another four slices in, buttered the ones that were done, and set them on top of an already tall pile on a plate. It seemed like she was making enough to feed a small army.

Scout strolled in and gave Cat a quick pat on her butt. "How's breakfast coming along, Kitty Cat?"

"Better now that the princess is finally up," she grumbled.

"Well then, I'm glad Blue's around to lend a hand in the kitchen."

"Blue?" Cat echoed softly.

"Yeah, she needed a nickname and Blue seemed like the obvious choice with those gorgeous eyes of hers," Scout explained.

If looks could kill, I'd have dropped dead on the spot after the venomous scowl Cat shot my way. She smiled up at Scout when he looked down at her, so he didn't catch the look she gave me. While he snagged a piece of toast before heading out the door, she pulled a couple of baking sheets of bacon out of the oven.

"You make your bacon in the oven?"

My question earned me another glare and an eye-roll. "Yeah, 'cause it's less messy and easier to cook it in big batches that way than in a pan." She gave me a considering look, and then her lips tilted up in a smug grin. "Although I guess that for the short time you're around, I don't have to worry about making a mess since I've got you to clean it up for me."

Ignoring her effort to push my buttons yet again, I asked a question that had been bugging me instead. "The old ladies in my dad's club don't take care of even half the stuff that you do. They hand most of it off to the girls who hang around for the guys. Couldn't you do the same and have them help you more often?"

"It isn't your job to question the way we do things around here," she spat at me. Then she slammed one of the empty baking sheets into the sink and stalked towards me. When she got close enough to reach me, she grabbed my upper arm and her nails dug into my skin. "The Silver Saints aren't anything like the Hounds of Hellfire, and we never will be. Why in the hell would we want to be when one of those motherfuckers put one of our guys in a coma for standing up for a woman?"

"I didn't—" My sentence broke off when she shook me.

"Of course you didn't! How could you when sheltered princesses don't know what goes on in the real world?" She swept her free hand in the air, waving around the kitchen. "Look around. Your daddy isn't here to protect you. Nobody is. Not even Mac. You might be wearing his cut, but that's only because he doesn't want the guys to take things too far with you. You're a commodity to him, nothing more. The lever he needed to pull to get your dad to come to the bargaining table. Nothing less, and sure as fuck nothing more. Not like it'll be when he finds the woman he wants to be his old lady and has her wear it. Assuming she'll even want the same one he put on your boney ass."

I'd held firm through her whole rant—right up until the point when she mentioned some other woman wearing Mac's cut. My mind filled with thoughts of someone else where I wanted to be. In his bed. Making a life with him. I yanked my arm out of Cat's hold. Once I was free, I ran out of the kitchen, through the bar area in front, and out the door.

If I hadn't been so upset, I would have heard the familiar rumble of engines as a group of motorcycles pulled in front of the clubhouse. But instead, I stumbled down the steps and onto the driveway with tears clouding my vision.

I heard Mac yell my name, and I stopped to rub at my eyes. He sounded weird. Pissed...and scared, maybe? My head popped up, and my heart raced in my chest when I saw two motorcycles barreling towards me. Before I had the chance to move, strong arms wrapped around my waist and lifted me out of harm's way.

"Shit," Mac grunted in my ear, squeezing me tight against his chest before setting me back on my feet. "That was too fucking close. What the hell were you thinking?" He shook me a little and scowled fiercely when he let go and saw red fingerprints and scratches on the arm Cat had grabbed in the kitchen. "Fuck, did I do that?"

His pale green eyes filled with remorse. I reached up and patted his chest softly. "No," I reassured him. "My skin is sensitive and marks easily, but this isn't from you."

The guilt bled out of his gaze and was replaced with fury. "Someone dared to touch you? Who was it?"

I stared up at him and shook my head. "It's nothing. Just the way my skin is. Don't worry about it."

His fingers gripped the edges of his cut and pulled me into his chest. "I'm the Prez. You're wearing my patch. That means you're untouchable. But you've got marks on your arm, tears in your eyes, and you almost got run down by one of my men. That sure as fuck is something."

I shook my head again. If I ever wanted any hope of a relationship with Mac in the future, I'd have to find a way to coexist with Cat. Things with her were bad enough, I didn't want to make them worse.

A frustrated growl rumbled up his chest, and I patted him gently again. His gaze dropped to my hand and filled with determination. Then he grabbed me around the waist, hoisted me over his shoulder, and stalked into the clubhouse.

Chapter Seven

Mac

I WAS SO DONE with this shit. One day...I'd only lasted one day. I knew it was pathetic but I was beyond caring at this point. My body was vibrating with tension—first from fear as I watched those bikes racing towards Bridget, then fury at the motherfucker who marked her beautiful skin, and now I was consumed by lust. Everything had come together and combusted, blowing apart my good intentions.

Cat was standing in the doorway watching, her eyes wide, and she had to jump out of the way so I wouldn't run into her.

Bridget tugged on the back of my shirt, no doubt close to where her face was currently hanging. "Um…where are we going?" Her voice was hesitant, but with a thread of heated excitement.

I patted her ass and then used a firm hand to hold her steady as I jogged up the stairs. "You know exactly what's happening here, Bridget," I growled. "I'm done fighting this. Us. I fucking need you."

"Okay!" she squeaked. I chuckled as I barged through my bedroom door and slammed it shut. Then I tossed her on the bed and came down over her. Her soft body melted under mine, and I groaned.

Somehow this slip of a girl had tossed my world upside down and then righted it, when I hadn't even realized it had always been crooked.

I lowered my head and sucked lightly on her bottom lip before sealing our mouths together in a deep kiss. My tongue swept inside, and I grunted in approval when hers timidly tangled with mine.

"You taste like fucking heaven, baby," I mumbled as I placed hot, wet kisses along her jaw and down the long column of her throat. She moaned and the sound shot through me, taking the little blood I had left in my brain straight to my groin.

I pulled back, just a little, and took in the sight of her sprawled on my bed, wearing my cut. A declaration that she was mine. In that moment, I knew, I'd have to figure out another way to bargain with Pierce. Bridget wasn't going anywhere; I was keeping her. Age be damned. Fuck the rivalry with her father. Screw anything and everything that might keep me from her. I'd steamroll over anything in my way.

Part of me wanted to take things sweet and slow for her, but I was still amped up from almost seeing her mowed down and the fury at the bruising and scratches on her arms.

I practically ripped the clothes from her body and then quickly shucked my own. Fuck, but she was beautiful. All pale, creamy skin, with a sprinkling of freckles that I couldn't wait to connect with my tongue. Rosy nipples puckered on her generous tits, begging for my mouth. Her blue eyes were wide and glazed with desire, while her flaming red hair was spread out around her like a halo of fire.

Gathering her tight to me, I hissed out a breath at the electricity that sizzled everywhere our naked skin touched. Her hands caressed my face before delving into my hair and yanking my face down so she could claim a deep kiss. I couldn't help a small chuckle at her attempt at being aggressive. It was cute as fuck and yet, also incredibly sexy.

I shifted so my throbbing cock was nestled in the curls at the juncture of her thighs. Her pussy was hot, and I slid through her wetness as it coated the underside of my dick. I wanted so badly to bury myself fast and hard inside her, but her obvious innocence caused me to hesitate.

"Are you a virgin, baby?" I asked gruffly. I was pretty sure I knew her answer but I asked anyway, to be certain. I wanted her either way, but if some other motherfucker had touched my woman, I would hunt him down and wipe her from his memory.

A sweet blush stole over her face, spreading down over her chest. She nodded shyly and squirmed underneath me. "Don't move like that, Bridget," I snapped. She froze, and I immediately attempted to soften my tone. "I don't want to lose control and be too rough with you, baby."

Her blush intensified and her eyes dropped to my chest, staring intently at my ink. "What if I want you to lose control? To be raw and real with me?"

Fucking hell. This woman was perfect. So innocent and seemingly shy. But there was a wildcat hiding in there, I was sure of it. It was going to become my mission in life to get her to open up and be comfortable being herself.

"Gotta be gentle with you this first time. Don't worry, someone is going to lose control,"—I grinned—"it just won't be me." I was determined and little cocky, completely confident in my ability to hold back. I'd never given myself to a woman completely. I'd never give up that level of control.

I didn't wait for her to respond, instead I set about my goal starting with her deliciously tempting nipples. I sucked each peak in turn, lavishing them with my tongue and scraping them gently through my teeth. Then I kissed my way down her body until I was nestled between her thighs. "Been craving another taste of this pussy. Haven't been able to get it out of my mind." Since I would have to be careful when it came time to put my cock in her, I allowed myself to go a little crazy with my mouth at her core. I tongue-fucked her hard, reveling in her moans and shivers. Then I pumped her with two fingers while I feasted on her clit. It didn't take long to drive her over the edge, and I lapped up every bit of her juices as she screamed my name.

Part of me could have stayed there all day, making her come over and over with my mouth and hand. But my cock was leaking heavily and painfully hard.

I climbed back up and slid my cock through her drenched pussy again, getting it good and wet, knowing her slickness would make getting my large dick inside her a little easier.

Slowly, I eased the tip in and already her pussy began squeezing. "Fuck, you're tight," I grunted. "Put your legs around me, baby." She did as she was told, and I slid in another inch. I worked myself in slowly, allowing her to adjust to my size before moving deeper. By the time I was fully seated inside her, I was dripping with sweat from my efforts to hold back.

"Jared," Bridget moaned as she writhed and her inner muscles clenched.

I fucking lost it. I pulled out, almost all the way, and then thrust in fast and hard until I was balls deep again. I felt mindless with lust as I repeated the action, increasing in speed and pounding my cock in her pussy. Her screams of pleasure fed my need for her and I shoved her legs up so her knees went to her chest. The new angle allowed me to slide in even deeper, and I shouted at the overwhelming sensation.

I tried to keep a thread of sanity about me, to make sure I wasn't hurting her. But her hips bucked, meeting me thrust for thrust, her mouth opened and her head was thrown back in ecstasy.

"I could live inside your pussy, baby." I growled. "That's right, squeeze the fuck out of my cock. Take every fucking inch."

"Yes! Jared. Yes!" she cried out.

I was close, I could feel the telling tingle in my spine. I leaned down and sucked on her nipples as my fingers deftly found her bundle of nerves and pushed her higher. Suddenly her whole body tensed and she shattered with an ear-splitting scream.

My cock exploded with my release as my roar of surrender practically shook the walls. I kept a steady rhythm, my cock filling her so full of my come it was spilling from her womb. To my shock, Bridget exploded once more and it set off another small orgasm in me. I would have thought my dick was thoroughly empty, but the ejaculations just kept on pulsing.

Finally, I began to soften as Bridget's shudders subsided and our heart rates slowed. Fucking A. I'd never experienced anything like this, it was fucking intense.

I stared down at her gorgeous face in silence for a few minutes. Her eyes were closed and her face was filled with blissful contentment.

This had changed everything, and I had to make sure she was completely aware. "Baby, look at me," I gruffed. Her eyes opened languidly, the blue orbs hazy with afterglow. "There's no turning back, Bridget," I told her seriously. "This means you're mine. Do you understand that? I won't be letting you go."

Chapter Eight

B ridget

APPARENTLY, the third time was the charm when it came to my stay with the Silver Saints because I found myself wrapped tight in Mac's arms after waking up. I was still exhausted, but incredibly grateful to not have overslept and missed out on the experience. Although we'd spent most of the previous day in bed, we'd barely gotten any sleep—but I'd certainly gotten an extremely thorough introduction into passion. Mac had wrung orgasm after orgasm out of my body until we both collapsed. Shifting in Mac's arms, I felt the impact of how we'd spent that time in muscles I hadn't even known I had.

That didn't stop me from reaching out to gently trace the inked lines on his skin like I'd always wanted to do. Or from rubbing my cheek against his beard, the rough glide reminding me of all the places where my skin had beard burn. And it certainly didn't make me reconsider tugging the sheet lower until his hard length popped free from where it had been tenting the material. I peeked up at his face to find his eyes still closed and his face relaxed. Trailing my fingers down his six-pack abs, I slowly wiggled out of his arms. Then I rose up on my knees and lowered my head to lick at the bead of moisture on the tip of his cock. Mac's low groan when my tongue stroked against his heated flesh had my head jerking back up. His pale green eyes were open, alert...and focused on me.

"You wake up hungry for me, baby?"

"Hungry?" I echoed.

My gaze followed the movement of his hand as he reached down to grip his cock and stroke it. "You wanna wrap those lips of yours around my cock the same way I'm starving for a taste of your sweet little pussy?"

"Yes. Yes, I do." I licked my lips, watching his

hand move up and down. I couldn't tear my eyes away because it was ridiculously sexy. Even after all the orgasms he'd given me, I was more turned on than I'd ever been before. Watching what he was doing made me more than hungry for him; that was for sure.

His free hand slid up my thigh, under the shirt I was wearing. It was one of his, and it hit me mid-thigh. I'd pulled it on before passing out, not bothering with panties, so his touch met nothing but bare skin. "Then come sit on my face so we can both get what we want."

With a nudge on my hip, he guided me towards his shoulders. Moving carefully, I straddled them with my pussy right over his head. He shoved the shirt up and over my hips so I was fully exposed to his gaze. The position made me feel vulnerable, and a deep flush washed over my skin.

"Lower, baby. Settle that pretty pussy right over my mouth so I can get my taste."

I nearly moaned at the sensual command in his tone as I inched my hips lower. My legs trembled at the first swipe of his tongue, and I had to brace a hand on Mac's thigh before I collapsed on top of his body. He lapped at me, and my hips chased his mouth as I lost all train of thought.

He gripped the base of his cock to aim it at my lips. "Don't forget you were going to get a taste too, baby. I want to feel those lips wrapped around my cock while I fuck you with my tongue."

"It's your fault I forgot what I was doing," I laughed. "You're too darn good at what you're doing to me."

"It's a good thing you think so because I plan on eating this pussy all the fucking time."

"Oh my," I sighed as he went back to it. Before I lost the ability to do anything but scream in ecstasy, I lowered my head to run my tongue around the crown of his cock. When I opened my mouth wide over his length, his hips bucked upwards. He was in control of both of our pleasure, with his mouth eating at me while he fed me his cock. He kept one hand wrapped around the base, and the other dug into my hip as he pulled me down so his mouth could reach my clit. When his lips closed around it and tugged, I exploded. Whimpering around a mouthful of cock, I rode my orgasm out while he continued to pump in and out of my mouth until he yanked me off and came on my chest in spurts.

When his cock stopped twitching, I flopped onto my back on the mattress next to him. "We should wake up hungry more often." My stomach chose that moment to make a rumbling noise, and Mac's followed suit. I burst into a fit of giggles, laughing even harder when his low chuckle echoed around me. "I guess I'd better get up and hit the kitchen. Get us some real food."

"Stay in bed and rest. I'll let Cat know that you aren't up to helping this morning."

"I want to," I reassured him. "Gotta feed my man since he can't survive—"

"On just your delicious pussy alone," he finished for me with a grin.

I shook my head and rolled my eyes, blushing as I hopped off the mattress and headed into the bathroom to clean up. When I came back out, Mac was gone. But he'd left a pair of jeans, one of his shirts, and his cut for me on the bed. I pulled on the clothes and went to the kitchen, coming up short when Cat flashed me a genuine smile.

"Morning," I greeted her cautiously, more than a little weirded out by her reaction to me since it was the opposite of how she'd been treating me ever since Mac had brought me here. Then her eyes darted to the bruises and scratches she'd left on me the day before, and I figured she was feeling guilty. "It looks way worse than it should because I bruise easily."

"You have every right to hate me since I've been a royal bitch to you," she started.

"I don't hate you." I moved closer, shaking my head. "I mean, yeah, you were a total bitch. But I get it with how the situation is between the Silver Saints and the Hounds of Hellfire."

"Which is exactly why I expected you to tell Mac that it was my fault. All of it."

"All of what?" Scout growled from behind me. I twirled around and found him glaring at Cat.

"I—"

"It's nothing," I interrupted.

"Didn't sound like nothing to me," he argued. "Is Blue right, Kitty Cat?"

"No," she whispered, her voice sounding uncertain and lacking her usual confidence.

"One of you'd better tell me what the fuck is going on."

"The bruises and scratches on Bridget's arms are my fault," Cat blurted out.

Scout lifted one of my wrists to examine the marks on my skin. "Mac was pissed as fuck about these."

"Yeah," I admitted softly.

"He didn't know how they happened, though."

"Because she didn't tell," Cat said. "Just like she

didn't say anything about how I made her run outta here crying yesterday when I ripped her to shreds."

"Shit, Kitty Cat," he groaned. "What the fuck were you thinking?"

"That she was a pawn who didn't deserve my respect. A pampered princess who didn't belong here, and I was stuck with her until her father finally caves and gives Mac what he wants."

"You're my old lady. You know me. Would I ever give someone a nickname if I didn't think they deserved my respect?" he asked.

Cat shook her head.

He jabbed a finger at the patch on Mac's cut. "You, better than any other woman around here, should know what it means for Mac to give her that to wear."

Cat cringed. "I know, which is why I never should have told her—"

"It doesn't matter what was said," I interrupted again, but for a different reason this time. I didn't want to hear a repeat of the insults she'd flung at me yesterday, especially the ones about some other woman wearing Mac's cut in the future. Not after spending all day and night in his bed.

Scout gave me a considering look. "My woman and I don't keep secrets from each other."

I gave him a disbelieving look because we both knew darn well that with club business being what it was, there were things he kept from her.

"Not with shit like this," he growled.

"It's girl stuff. None of your concern," I insisted, putting a little bit of haughtiness in my tone. "Besides which, it's over and done with so there's nothing to worry about. Cat and I are good with each other."

He shifted his gaze to Cat. "You good with Blue now, Kitty Cat?"

"Damn straight." She nodded as she stepped to my side, presenting a united front. "From now on, I've got Blue's back the same way she had mine."

"Good," Scout grunted. "That's the way it should be since you're the VP's old lady and she's the Prez's."

The Prez's old lady. Wow. Getting kidnapped by Mac really was the best thing that'd ever happened to me.

Chapter Nine

Mac

I WANTED nothing more than to spend another day lost in Bridget's delicious body, but I had shit to do. Not the least of which was coming up with a new plan. Pierce wasn't getting his daughter back, so I needed a new way to get ahold of the asshole who'd beat up my guy.

Sitting at my desk, I forced myself to focus on some paperwork until there was a soft knock at my door. "Yeah?" I called. Looking up, I felt a smile spread across my lips as Bridget came into the room with a tray full of food. Honestly, I was a little worried my face was going to break, I hadn't smiled this much in years.

I leaned back in my chair as she scooted in front of me to set the tray down, then grabbed her waist and hoisted her into my lap. Her squeak of surprise melted into a moan when I buried my face in her neck and nibbled on the soft flesh.

"I could get used to this," I mumbled. "Having you for first breakfast and then being served a second one by you while wearing my cut"—she giggled and squirmed, causing my already semi-hard cock to turn to steel—"If you don't stop wiggling, you'll be my morning snack too."

Grabbing her chin, I turned her head and captured her lips in a deep, hungry kiss. Things were starting to heat up when my door slammed open, bouncing off the wall. I scowled darkly at Scout as he sauntered into the room. "You forget how to fucking knock, Scout?"

Scout grinned unapologetically as Bridget scurried off my lap, her face colored pink. "I was just leaving."

I was tempted to tell Scout to fuck off and continue with Bridget, but I had shit to discuss with him. I was going to need his help figuring out how to handle the fucking mess I'd created by claiming Bridget.

"Come back at lunch, baby," I called before she shut the door quietly behind her.

Scout sprawled in a chair across from me and raised a brow. "I take it she's gonna be a permanent fixture around here from now on."

"Damn straight," I growled. "Anybody has a problem with that, they can leave their cut and get the fuck out."

"Whatever happed to 'bros before hoes,' man?" Scout scoffed.

He was teasing, and I didn't take the bait. "We aren't in second grade. Now, you ready to stop acting like it and get the fuck to work?"

"How you gonna handle the Hounds of Hellfire?"

I scrubbed my hands down my face and grunted in frustration. "No fucking clue."

Just then, my phone rang and I grabbed it, barking, "Prez."

"I've got your man," Pierce snapped on the other end of the line. "He's willing to turn himself in to the police."

"That's not how we handle this shit," I growled.

"Like I don't fucking know that. But taking my

baby girl was a step too far, Mac. You give her back to me, and I'll convince Gil to deal with you rather than the police."

Fuck. I was going to have to stall until I could figure out my next step. I wasn't going to let that motherfucking coward hide behind bars rather than face me. "Fine." Scout pushed a handwritten note across the desk. I glanced down to see a date and location. "At the Junction race on Saturday."

"Saturday!" Pierce sputtered. "That's way too fucking long for my girl to be locked up with your people! You'll break her!"

I almost laughed, but I didn't want to give away any kind of emotion in regards to Bridget. I couldn't help a parting shot though. "She's stronger than you think, old man." Then I hung up. "And she's mine."

Our treasurer, Link, joined us just then and I gave Scout a look to tell him to keep his mouth shut. Then the three of us got down to club business.

It was after three when I glanced at the clock. Bridget hadn't come back at lunch. I frowned, worry creeping in. There were so many ways for her to get into trouble or get hurt. Link left and I stood to follow him but stopped when Scout said my name.

"I'm sure she's with Cat, Mac. I need to talk to you for a minute."

My brows raised at his tone. He sounded almost hesitant, which was rare. I crossed my arms over my chest and stared at him, waiting.

"I walked in on a conversation between Bridget and Cat this morning," he started. He went on to explain everything about Bridget's bruises and what else had happened.

Fury burned in my gut, and I clenched my fists in an effort to expend some of my energy so I wouldn't blow the roof off with my temper.

"She was way outta line, brother," I growled.

Scout held up his hands in surrender. "She knows that, believe me. But she owned up to her mistakes and I think you'll find she'll have Bridget's back from now on."

I glared at him. "She fucking better. 'Cause she's on thin-fucking ice with me. If Bridget so much as—"

"She's good, Mac." Scout's eyes narrowed as he cut me off. "I told you because we don't keep secrets and shit, but you gotta trust me to handle my woman. Besides that, you know Cat. She's good."

I nodded, trying to let go of my anger. He was right, but I was having a hard time accepting it with the red haze of anger that came with the thought of Bridget being hurt, physically or verbally.

Scout took a step forward, his gray eyes probing mine. "Won't happen again. We good?"

I blew out a breath and nodded as I rounded the desk and headed for the door. "Yeah."

The first place I checked was the kitchen, but there were only a couple of guys sitting around the long, wooden table, talking and drinking. I headed to our room next but was waylaid by our enforcer, Dax, as I jogged up the stairs.

"Yo. Cat took your lady shopping."

I pivoted and descended the stairs before responding. "She what? Where?"

Dax shrugged. "Fuck if I know. I'm just relaying a message because Cat threatened to rip off my balls if I didn't let you know." He turned and began to walk away, shaking his head. "Don't know when I turned into such a pussy that I ended up a messenger boy instead of a bad ass fucking enforcer."

The corners of my mouth edged up as I made my way out to the garage to check on our latest order for custom bikes. We'd have to keep this shit on a leash and make sure that it never got around what suckers we were for our women.

"HI." A soft, sweet voice brought my head up fast and I cursed as my forehead slammed into the bike I was currently under.

"Are you okay?" Bridget's frantic voice came closer as I slid out from under the hog. She kneeled beside me, her blue eyes filled with worry.

I was about to tell her I was fine but the words caught in my throat as my eyes traveled over her. She was wearing a pink, sleeveless top that had a V in the front, showing a hint of her luscious cleavage. It clung to her in all the right places, and my mouth began to water while my fingers itched to tug it down and bare her gorgeous tits.

Her tiny, denim shorts that made her legs look a mile long, and I had a feeling they cupped her pert little ass perfectly. She glowed with confidence and smiled as she watched me ogle her.

"Where's my cut?" I growled. It came out sounding grittier than I'd intended, due to my suddenly lust-consumed state. Her eyes filled with hurt, and I instantly wanted to slam my fist into my own face. I should have complimented her first and not been so harsh when I did finally say something. But damn, this woman kept throwing me off balance.

"You look absolutely gorgeous, baby," I told her as I ran a finger down her velvety cheek. "But, I told you, you always gotta be wearing my mark. It keeps you safe."

Her smile returned, though somewhat timidly, and she reached for a bag she'd set near her feet. "Sorry, I forgot to put it back on." She dug through the contents then pulled my leather vest from the depths and quickly donned it.

"Now you look *too* fucking good, baby." I grinned and her cheeks dusted with pink as her smile grew. "Cat took you shopping?" I growled playfully and dragged her into my lap to kiss the fuck out of her. "I like seeing you in my clothes."

She giggled and pulled back to gaze up at me. "As much as I like wearing your clothes, they aren't very practical for me since you're practically twice my size." The pink in her cheeks spread over her whole face and she ducked her head and mumbled something.

I put a finger under her chin and lifted her face. "Didn't understand that, baby."

She cleared her throat and glanced away but forced her eyes back to mine before speaking. "I—um—also got some stuff…you know, just for you." Then she gestured to a pink striped bag hiding behind the one I'd seen next to her.

I jumped to my feet and tossed her over my

shoulder, then scooped up the bags and raced for the clubhouse, Bridget giggling all the way.

Just as I entered, I almost ran into Dax. "Gotta talk, Prez."

"Later," I barked as I tried to move around him.

He grabbed my arm, and I spun around with a murderous scowl.

"Hospital called. Logan's awake."

Chapter Ten

B ridget

"THANK FUCK," Mac sighed as he set me on my feet before swatting me on my ass, hard enough that I felt it but not so much that it hurt. "Gimme a second, baby."

"Okay, I'll take these"—I grabbed the bags out of his hand, shuffling the one with the lingerie I'd purchased to the back as I blushed—"and meet you up in your room."

"Ours, Bridget," Mac corrected.

The guy who stopped us looked as confused as I felt.

"Huh?" I asked.

He lifted a hand and traced along my collarbone and down my chest where his cut rested. "You're wearing my mark, sleeping in my bed. I've claimed you, baby. That makes *my* room *our* room."

"Oh! Right. Yeah," I mumbled, trying to keep my cool when all I wanted to do was jump for joy.

"Fucking adorable." I peeked up to find him smiling down at me with a knowing grin. "Take your shit up to our room while I talk to Dax."

I did as he asked, dumping my shopping bags on the bed before heading into the bathroom to freshen up. My outing to the mall with Cat brought a whole new meaning to the phrase "shop 'til you drop." I'd been surprised by how well the VP's old lady knew her way around all the best stores. And then surprise turned to shock when she'd dragged me into Victoria's Secret to help me pick out sexy stuff that was "guaranteed to bring Mac to his knees," as she'd put it.

I'd been a little uncomfortable at first, but she'd been so darn excited to help me that I'd gone with it anyway. And once I'd pictured Mac's reaction to me in the scraps of black lace that she'd shoved into my hands before pushing me into a changing room, I'd become eager to try on all sorts of things I'd never have considered before. When we'd left the store, I couldn't wait to get back to the Silver Saints compound so I could show Mac everything I'd bought. Unfortunately, when I walked out of the bathroom and saw the stony look on his face, I knew I was going to have to wait before I'd have the chance to model it all for him.

"Shit, baby," he groaned, pulling me into his strong arms. "If this wasn't so damn important, I'd fuck that look of disappointment right off your face. But we've been waiting to be able to talk to one of my guys who's in the hospital, and one of the prospects called to let me know that Logan's finally awake. I've gotta head to the hospital, and it can't wait."

I thought back to what I'd overheard when Mac called my dad the day he'd taken me. "The one in the coma?"

"Yup."

"Because of something someone in the Hounds of Hellfire did?" I whispered.

"One of those motherfuckers beat the shit out of my Road Captain with a baseball bat because he didn't like it when Logan stepped in when he was roughing up a woman."

"No," I gasped in shock. I knew the guys in my dad's club weren't model citizens, but I couldn't picture one of them doing that. Going after another guy with a baseball bat in a fit of rage? Maybe. Knocking a woman around? No way. "Are you sure that's what happened? My dad would never put up with one of his guys hitting a woman."

"I've got zero doubt about it, Bridget. Neither does your dad. He knows which of his men put Logan in the hospital, and he hasn't done jack shit to make it right."

"No." I shook my head, refusing to believe that was true. "My dad wouldn't do that."

"I'm sorry, baby, but he did. I talked to him myself this morning."

Ducking my head as my eyes filled with tears, Mac pulled me into his arms. Although I didn't know any details because it was club business, I was aware that my dad did things that weren't legal. I had been ever since kindergarten when some of my classmates' parents didn't want them to be my friend because of who my dad was. It'd never really bothered me since I was well loved by him. If other people wanted me to choose between them and my dad, there was no contest. But that was before Mac. I didn't know what I'd do if I ever had to choose between the two most important men in my life.

"C'mon. You're coming to the hospital with me."

"Are you sure?" I sniffled.

His arms tightened around me briefly, and then he set me away. Looking down at me, he swiped his thumbs over my cheeks to wipe away my tears. "I'm not gonna leave you alone when you're like this. I should have kept my damn mouth shut. That shit is between your dad and me. Between the Hounds of Hellfire and the Silver Saints. It doesn't have anything to do with you."

"You kidnapped me because of it," I reminded him.

"That was then. This is now."

He must have considered the conversation closed because he led me out the door and to his bike. As soon as I was settled behind him, with the helmet he'd given me securely in place, we roared away from the clubhouse with several of the guys following behind us. It took us about fifteen minutes to make it to the hospital, but it hadn't been long enough for me to come to terms with the idea that my dad was the bad guy in this situation. So, I was quiet as Mac led the way upstairs to Logan's hospital room, his hand wrapped around mine to keep me close. He only let go when we were through the door and he walked to the side of the hospital bed. In it was a man with shaggy blond hair and blue eyes on a heavily bruised face. One of his legs was casted and in traction, and the arm on the opposite side was in a sling. He gave me a curious look before switching his gaze to Mac and offering him a sheepish grin.

"How long was I out?" he asked.

"About a week," Mac answered.

"That's what they told me." Logan's blue eyes slid my way again. "But then I saw you holding hands like a sap, and I figured it'd been long enough that hell froze over."

I giggled at the joke, but Mac just glared at him. "Too early for you to joke about being in a fucking coma, man. I was starting to think you'd never wake up."

"Sorry, Prez. I guess I'm still trying to wrap my head around the fact that I got my ass beat so bad by a motherfucking Hound of Hellfire that I missed an entire week of my life."

I cringed at the reminder of my dad's involvement in this man ending up in the condition he was in, but neither man seemed to notice and the other guys were behind me and couldn't see my face.

"But don't worry, I'll more than make up for lost time once I get my hands on him."

"Ahem," Scout cleared his throat, stepping next to me and jerking his head in my direction.

"Can you go get Logan some water, baby? I'm sure he's thirsty," Mac asked.

I knew he was trying to get me out of the room, but with the direction the conversation had turned I was glad for the excuse. "Sure."

"Make it ice chips, sweetheart," Logan said. Mac growled at him, moving so his view of me was blocked. "I didn't mean anything by it, Prez. Don't know the girl's name and didn't know what else to call her."

"Blue," Scout offered. "You can call her Blue."

"Works for me," Logan muttered. "I'm thirsty as fuck, but the doc won't let me have anything but ice chips. So if Blue could grab me some, I'd be grateful."

"Will do," I called out as I hurried out of the room. The nurses' station was right around the corner, so it didn't take me long to get what Logan needed. When I made it back to his room, the door was only cracked open about an inch but I could hear the low murmur of male voices. I started to open my mouth to make sure they knew I was there, but then what Mac was saying hit me and I froze in my tracks.

"Pierce called this morning. He's willing to make the trade. Their guy for Bridget."

"Damn, this situation is fucked since Bridget's

the chick you looked like you were going to put me back in my coma for after I called her sweetheart. What'd you tell him?" Logan asked.

"What the fuck did you think I said? I gave him the time and place for the meet. This Saturday at the races."

"No," I mouthed, my eyes welling with tears. Swiveling on my foot, I dropped the pitcher of ice as I ran quickly. I needed to be alone. Needed to figure out what to think. One question kept echoing in my mind. *Had he been playing me the whole time?*

Chapter Eleven

Mac

ALL EYES SWUNG to the partially open door when something clattered and bounced off the linoleum floor. I only caught a glimpse of Bridget's expression before she took off, but it was enough for me to see her blue eyes swimming with hurt.

"Shit."

Scout waved at the door. "Go, we got this."

I nodded, already running into the hallway. "Bridget!" I roared. I caught up to her just as she burst into the waiting room. Snatching her wrist, I hauled her back up against me, lifting her feet clear off the floor.

"Let me go!" she snapped, wiggling frantically.

"No." My tone was hard as I spoke quietly into her ear. Just the thought of losing her had me on edge. "I already told you, you're mine." Her shoulders slumped but she settled a little so I cautiously set her down.

The room was littered with my brothers and a few old ladies, so I led Bridget back into the hallway and found a deserted hospital room.

When I faced her, my heart pounded painfully at the sight of tears streaming down her beautiful face. "Don't ever run from me, baby," I growled. "You hear something you don't like or understand, you come to me. That's how this is gonna work. Do I make myself clear?"

She backed away and I stifled the urge to make a grab for her. "What do you care? I'm just leverage." Her back straightened and she glared at me. "I'm not going to be your plaything until you've found a better use for me."

I closed the distance between us in one step and grasped her face, forcing her to look up at me. "Don't ever refer to yourself as my plaything, baby, or I'll be bending you over my knee." I took a deep breath and tried to calm myself. "My old lady, my woman, and someday my wife; those describe what you are to me."

Her blue eyes went wide as saucers and her jaw dropped. I couldn't resist dipping my head and stealing a fast kiss.

"But...what about...?"

"I needed time to come up with another method to get what I need from your dad, baby. Only agreed to stall him. You aren't going fucking anywhere without me." I walked her backwards until she was pressed against the wall. "Pretty sure I made it very clear who you belong to the last couple of days. But, I'm more than happy to remind you."

I captured her lips in a deep kiss, my palms planted on either side of her head. My hips grinded into her center, making it abundantly clear what she did to me.

My hands slid into her hair, before continuing on and making quick work of the front snap on her shorts. I shoved them down, along with her panties, and hoisted her up with my hands under her ass.

Spinning around, I stalked to the nearest bed and set her on the edge before dropping to my knees between her legs. I inhaled deeply. "Fuck, you smell good. Taste so fucking good." Leaning in, I blew on her wet pussy, before licking up her slit. Bridget moaned and fell back onto her elbows, keeping herself elevated just enough that she could watch me. "Good girl. Eyes on me." I smirked then focused on my task of making her come. My tongue fucked her sweet pussy, my lips sucked hard at her clit, but just as she approached the peak, I backed off.

She whimpered and shuddered, looking at me in disbelief. "Tell me who you belong to, baby, and I'll let you come."

"You," she breathed.

"Fuck yes," I grunted. This time, when I drove her up, I pushed her right over the edge, soaking in the sounds of her passionate cries.

I surged to my feet and freed my cock, thrusting deep inside her before she'd even recovered.

"Jared," she gasped. "Yes!"

The sound of her sweet voice calling my name was like fuel on the fire. I held her hips tight as I pounded inside her. I ripped her shirt over her head and bending forward, my lips captured a nipple. I sucked hard, causing her to buck against me.

It didn't take long for her to explode again and I followed behind her, shouting her name. Still holding her firmly, I pressed our centers together, keeping it sealed so none of my seed would leak out.

"Don't ever forget you're mine, Bridget," I

mumbled, my face nestled between her tits. "Hopefully, you've already got my baby in your belly to prove it. If not, gonna fuck you every chance I get until you do."

"Oh my gosh!" she gulped. "We haven't been using protection!"

I lifted my head and glared at her. "Fuck no, we haven't. And we aren't gonna start now."

"You—you want me to have your baby?" she stuttered.

"Hell yes. Gonna have all my babies." I grinned this time, my smile growing wider when her face softened despite her obvious attempt to look like a bad ass. It was already a futile effort, considering she was still spread out on the bed with my dick buried deep in her pussy.

"Just exactly how many babies are you expecting me to have?"

I kissed her quickly before slowly pulling out. "As many as you're willing to give me."

She practically melted and I laughed as I helped her redress her boneless body. "Okay," she sighed dreamily.

After we were both dressed, I took her hand and led her towards the door but stopped when she tugged on my hand.

"What are we going to do about...that guy?" Her eyes had turned sad, so I held back from reminding her the shithead she was referring to was *her Dad's* guy.

"I'll handle it, baby. Trust me."

Her hand tightened in mine and she nodded determinedly. "I trust you."

I smiled again and gave in to the instinct to kiss her. Then we left the room and headed back to Logan, who was still talking with Scout. Dax, Link, and a couple of other brothers had joined in the discussion.

Holding Bridget with an arm around her waist, I made my way over to Logan's bed.

He craned his neck to look around me. "Sorry about what you heard, Blue." My eyebrows shot up at Logan's apology. He hadn't done anything wrong. I almost laughed when I realized it was simply the effect Bridget had on us all. Turned us into fucking pussies.

She smiled and shrugged. "My fault for jumping to conclusions. Besides, I understand why you'd still want Mac to use me as leverage. I want that guy to pay too."

Logan frowned and I figured he was about to correct her about wanting to use her but she continued on, "Maybe you guys should still use me."

"The fuck!" I exploded. "You're not leaving me. You need another reminder, baby?" I growled.

"No," she squeaked, her cheeks burning brightly with a deep blush. "I just meant that we could use me as a sort of bait. You kidnapped me once, may—"

"Not fucking happening, Bridget. So just forget that shit right now."

Logan interrupted, "We've got another idea, Prez. If Pierce can get Gil—"

"Gil?" Bridget asked, her nose scrunching up like she smelled something bad. "Figures it was him."

I raised an eyebrow and waited for her to explain.

"He's bad news. My dad always warned me to stay far away from him. If he was with a girl, it was probably Lena. She's been his on again, off again for a few years."

"If she was with the group. Think you could point her out to us, baby?" I asked.

She nodded. "Sure. She's really beautiful. Gil likes to show her off, so when they are together, he usually brings her with him wherever he goes."

"We can get to Gil another way, Mac," Logan said. "All I want is to talk to Lena, away from him."

"I can make that happen," Bridget smiled confidently as she spoke. "Bring Cat and I'll have her 'bump' into Lena and spill something. When she comes to the ladies room, I'll be waiting to talk to her."

The idea of Bridget anywhere near any of the Hounds of Hellfire had my fists clenching in rage. But, I knew we needed her and anyone of my men would throw down their life to protect her. I sighed and agreed to the new plan.

I ROARED Bridget's name as I bucked up and came inside her again. After I'd practically torn off her new lingerie, I'd taken her up against the wall then she'd ridden me hard. She was so fucking sexy.

Collapsing on my chest, she sighed contentedly. "Mac?" she whispered.

"Yeah, baby?"

"I...um, I know it's fast but I..." she trailed off and buried her face in my chest hair.

Fisting her hair, I tugged gently to lift her head. "Tell me you love me, Bridget." Her beautiful face flushed pink in the most adorable way. "Tell me," I demanded again.

"I love you." She smiled shyly and her hopeful blue eyes stared into mine.

"I love you too, baby."

Bridget lit up like the fucking sun and I immediately needed another taste of her sunshine.

Chapter Twelve

Bridget

"FUCK, I can't believe I agreed to this plan," Mac growled as he killed the engine on his bike. We'd just pulled up at the side of Knockers, one of the bars where the Hounds of Hellfire liked to hangout when they weren't at the clubhouse. With their scantily clad waitresses and cheap drinks, Knockers was popular with guys from other clubs too. It was considered neutral territory, but shit sometimes went down when clubs were already at odds with each other. Considering the current situation between my dad's club and the Silver Saints was volatile, I was hoping we'd be able to get in, get to Lena quickly, and get out before anything happened—and the only way that was going to happen was if Mac didn't show his face inside the bar.

"It'll be fine," I reassured him. "Out of everyone here, I'm in the least amount of danger because your guys would never hurt me and neither would my dad's."

"Promise me you won't take your safety for granted in there, baby. This whole fucking mess started because one of those motherfuckers was beating on a woman."

"Good point," I mumbled, patting his chest. "But I'm just going to duck inside and head straight to the restroom. Nobody should even see me."

"Just in case they do," he said as he reached behind him into the saddlebag. "I want you wearing this instead of my cut."

He pulled out a black leather vest, much smaller than his. Holding it up, he turned it around so I could see the back. Silver Saints MC was stitched at the top, and the patch below it said 'Property of Mac.' I knew what a big statement this was, and my eyes filled with tears. "Really?"

"Had it made just for you," he confirmed as he tugged his cut off my body and shrugged it on. "I love you. You love me." He claimed my mouth in a rough kiss and whispered the next words against my lips. "Been fucking you bare, which means you might already be carrying my baby. Want the whole damn world to know you're mine."

"This'll do it." I smiled up at him after pulling the vest on.

He rubbed his thumb along my ring finger on my left hand. "So will the ring I'm gonna put here soon."

"Oh, wow," I breathed out.

"So get your ass in there, do what's gotta be done, and come back out to me so we can get on with the rest of our lives."

"Yes, sir," I sassed back before turning on my heel and marching into the bar. It was dark inside, which was a good thing because it made it harder for the guys from the Hounds of Hellfire to notice me. I spotted them, though. Four of them were huddled together at a booth in the corner. A couple of pitchers of beer sat in front of them, mostly empty. When I glanced over at the bar, I spotted Lena. She was standing next to an empty stool, her toe tapping while she waited on the bartender.

Locking eyes with Cat, who was with a couple of other women at a table in the middle of the room, I jerked my chin in Lena's direction. Cat nodded, and I headed to the women's restroom. As the door swung shut, I heard a crashing sound and braced because I knew that it meant Cat had done her job and Lena would be right behind me.

"Bridget!" she gasped when she looked up from patting the wet spot on her shirt and spotted me.

I moved swiftly, slipping around her to block the door. "Hey, Lena."

"What're you doing here?" she asked, her eyes darting around like she expected someone to jump out at us. "Your dad's been going crazy since the Silver Saints took you. Did you escape? Do you need help?"

"I'm actually here to ask you the same question."

She gave me a confused look. "I don't understand. You were the one who was kidnapped out of your own bed. Not me. Why would I be the one who needed help?"

I lifted a finger and stroked it across the hint of a bruise on her cheekbone that wasn't quite covered by her makeup. Her eyes dropped to the floor, and I wanted to kick Gil's ass for taking so much of her confidence away from her. My dad, too, for letting him get away with it. But I was on a mission tonight, and I needed to focus on what needed to be done. "There's a guy in the hospital who got a lot more than that from Gil who wants to talk to you."

Her head jerked up and tears spilled down her cheeks. "I feel awful about what happened to him, but you know that I can't go and talk to him. Even without your dad being out for Silver Saint blood, Gil would never be okay with that."

"The choice is yours, Lena. Not theirs," I insisted. "And it's about time you realized it. I get being scared. Being used to doing what the guys say because it's what being with a Hounds of Hellfire means. But you deserve better than Gil."

She shrugged her shoulders helplessly. "I've tried walking away before, but somehow he's always managed to talk me into giving him another chance."

"Maybe it's finally time for you to leave him for good. Put a stop to the crap he's put you through and find someone who's better for you than he is…like the guy who defended you and ended up in a coma for it because Gil doesn't care about fighting fair. Not that it should be a surprise considering he also likes to hit women."

"Do you—" she broke off, shaking her head. "No, he couldn't possibly."

"Do I what, Lena?"

She took a deep breath and met my eyes hesitantly. "Do you really think that I could end up with a guy like the one who helped me?"

"Yeah, I do." I reached out and squeezed her hand. "And maybe not just with a guy *like* him."

"What do you mean?"

"Mac took me because he'd planned to do an exchange with my dad—me for Gil. But things have changed since then, and one of those things is that Logan woke up from his coma and what he wants more than a chance to beat the shit out of Gil is the opportunity to talk to you. So if you're willing to leave here with me now, the Silver Saints will let the matter drop with the Hounds of Hellfire."

"He's really willing to give up on his revenge? For me?" she squeaked.

"Yup."

"Wow."

"Yeah, wow. If I were in your shoes, it'd be a no brainer. Dump Gil for real this time. You don't even have to say a word to him. Just walk out of this bar, head over to the hospital, and see what kind of sparks fly between you and Logan. Even if nothing comes of it, the Silver Saints will make sure you're protected." Mac had made sure I knew that going into this, and it had only made me love him even more.

"He was pretty hot," she mumbled, blushing.

"Still is," I agreed, but only because Mac wasn't

around to hear me. "Even flat on his back and bruised the hell up."

She nodded, a determined light filling her eyes. "I'll do it."

"Hot damn!" I heaved a sigh of relief as I tugged on her hand. "Let's get out of here before anyone comes looking for you and finds me too."

The entire thing had gone more smoothly than I'd expected, but I got over-confident as we walked out of the bathroom and forgot to peek out to see if anybody was in the hallway. We only made it a few steps before I halted in my tracks. Lena bumped into me from behind and placed a hand at my back to steady herself. I glanced back at her when she gasped in surprise, and found her gaping down at the patch on my back instead of at the reason I'd stopped in the first place.

"Princess."

My head jerked forward again at the rasped out word.

"Daddy," I whispered. He looked like he hadn't slept the whole time I'd been gone, and I felt guilty because it'd been some of the best days of my life. I wanted to run forward and throw myself into his arms, but my feet felt like they were glued to the floor. It was a good thing, too, since I spotted Mac stalking towards us looking like he was ready to rip someone's head off.

"Oh, shit," Lena whispered.

She got that right. My dad led an unconventional life and was feared by many, but there had never been a moment of doubt in my life that he loved me. Then again, I'd never tested his love in the way I was about to do. God only knew how he was going to react to finding out I'd become Mac's old lady.

Chapter Thirteen

Mac

THE MINUTE I spied Pierce making his way towards the back of the bar, I hustled after him. There was a chance that he would end up in the bathroom before Lena and Bridget came out, but I wasn't holding my breath. It was clear the minute he saw her because he stopped suddenly, his whole body going stiff.

Bridget took a step towards her father but halted in her tracks when her eyes slid over his shoulder and met mine. Her hands went to the edges of her vest and she unconsciously tugged the leather tighter around her. If I hadn't been so pissed off at everything going to shit now, I would have smiled.

"Um, Daddy..." she trailed off hesitantly.

"Let's go, Princess." He reached out and grabbed her arm, making my vision go red. I didn't like anyone touching my woman and I didn't know if Pierce was truly a threat to her or not, which made it even worse.

"Don't fucking touch her," I growled before shoving him back and stepping in front of her.

Pierce's face started to turn purple with rage. "I brought you Gil, now give me my daughter, Mac. We had a deal."

I shook my head and gently pushed Bridget back behind me when I felt her try to peek around. "Deal is off. Gil can take his chances with the cops and Bridget goes home with me."

"You agreed—" Pierce started, but I cut him off.

"Gil has Bridget to thank. She talked my man into another solution."

"Bridget has nothing to do with club business, she can't change our deal," he said through a clenched jaw.

Slowly, I dragged Bridget around to my front, making sure she was facing me and pulling her hair forward so her back was unmistakably visible.

Pierce gasped and stumbled backwards. "What the fuck?" he roared.

"Bridget has everything to do with my club's business," I snarled. "As the president's old lady and as my soon to be wife, she's involved in whatever the hell I say she is."

"You can't force her to—"

"He isn't forcing me, Daddy." Bridget was the one cutting him off this time. She'd pushed lightly against my chest until I gave her a smidgen of room and then turned to face her father. "I love Mac and I'm choosing to stay at his side"—she squared her shoulders and straightened her back—"Besides, if anyone needs to learn a lesson about forcing women, it's the Hounds of Hellfire."

"Now you listen here, Bridget Pierce—"

I whistled loudly and made a "round 'em up" motion with my hand. Signaling to my guys who were waiting, unseen, just beyond the hallway. With one last glare at Pierce, I snapped, "I won't keep Bridget away from you, but if you want to see her or our children, you'll do it at the Silver Saints compound." With that, I spun around, keeping a firm hold on my woman so she was protected in front of me and we marched down the hall to the back entrance.

Bridget dug in her heels to get me to stop before I stepped outside and peered around me. "Lena?" she called. I glanced back to see the woman plastered up against the wall, looking like a deer in headlights. That's when I noticed two of my brothers restraining a man. He was cursing and trying to get free and come forward, scaring the shit out of Lena.

Scout brushed past them and swiftly walked over to Lena, he leaned down and whispered something to her and her whole body slumped. Then he placed a gentle hand on her shoulder and guided her in my direction.

Together, the four of us exited the building and made our way to the side where we'd parked our bikes. Cat strolled around from the front and gave me a chin lift before meeting Scout at his hog.

Cat had ridden her own bike at Bridget's suggestion and as soon as I saw her gesture to Lena to get on, I understood why. Lena had allowed Scout to lead her out of the building, but it was likely she wouldn't be very comfortable riding behind him.

My woman was fucking brilliant and gorgeous.

BRIDGET HELD Lena's arm and walked quietly

with her down the white-washed hallways of the hospital. Occasionally, Lena would whisper something and Bridget would either nod or shake her head. Finally, she pulled Lena to a stop outside Logan's room.

"I don't know if I should go in," Lena said, glancing warily at the door. "Are you sure he isn't mad at me? It's my fault he's here."

Bridget squeezed Lena's arm reassuringly. "I promise he wants to talk to you. And, I'm positive that it wasn't because he's mad." Bridget smirked. "I wouldn't be surprised if he uses your guilt to ask you for a sponge bath though..."

I threw my head back and laughed drawing the attention of both women. A sweet pink tinge appeared on Bridget's cheeks and I wanted nothing more than to return to the room we'd christened earlier. But, I knew Bridget didn't want Lena to face Logan alone, so I sighed and pushed the door open.

He was sitting up, a definite improvement from the last time we'd been here. The bruises and swelling on his face were also going down, though it would be a while before anyone would be commenting about his "pretty" face. Something we all loved to do to get a rise out of him.

When he spied our extra visitor, his face lit up

and he pushed away the small tray of food in front of him.

"You bring me someone special to kiss away my pain, Blue?" he asked with a lopsided grin.

Lena's eyes widened as she took in his appearance and her eyes filled with tears. That was my cue to get the fuck outta there.

"I'll be right outside when you're ready to go, baby," I whispered to Bridget before beating a hasty retreat.

Twenty minutes later, both women walked into the hall. Bridget was grinning ear to ear, and Lena was blushing like a virgin on prom night. I didn't ask for details, just grabbed ahold of my girl and headed home.

Epilogue

Bridget

STARING at my reflection in the bathroom mirror, I cringed. I was still in my pajamas. My hair was months overdue for a cut. I looked like I hadn't slept in forever. And I didn't have the energy to do more than run a brush through my hair and put on some lip gloss.

I felt like a mess, and it wasn't entirely due to my lack of sleep. It was because my dad was coming to the compound for the first time since Mac had thrown down the gauntlet almost eleven months ago in the hallway at Knockers. I'd talked to him on the phone and even met him out for meals a couple of times when I'd managed to sweet-talk Mac into it, but my dad hadn't seen fit to come visit me here yet. Until today...when Mac didn't give him any other choice.

My dad wanted to meet his new granddaughter, and it wasn't going to happen anywhere else other than the Silver Saints compound. It had taken him seven weeks—and lot of texts with ridiculously adorable photos of Molly—to finally concede the fact that Mac wasn't going to budge on this. Now that the day was finally here, I was freaking out.

"You almost ready?" Strong arms wrapped around me, and I lifted my gaze to meet Mac's eyes in the mirror. He rubbed his chin against my neck, his beard scraping against my tender skin and leaving goosebumps in its wake.

"I just need to change out of my pajamas. Other than that, I think this is about as good as its going to get today," I sighed.

He turned my head to the side to capture my lips in a deep kiss that left me wanting more when he pulled away. "That's bullshit. You need me to show you how fucking gorgeous you are?"

"Maybe," I breathed out. "But it's going to have to wait because we don't have enough time right now."

"And that's bullshit, too." He gripped my hips and flipped me around before setting me on the countertop. "Molly isn't crying."

He yanked my sleep shorts and panties down my legs. "Your dad isn't here yet."

Sinking a finger inside me, he growled, "You're already wet for me."

"After that kiss, of course I am."

His finger continued to work me as he used his other hand to unbuckle his belt, unsnap his jeans, slide the zipper down, and pull out his cock. "And I'm always hard for you."

I widened my legs so he could step between them. His hands moved to my hips, and he lined himself up at my entrance. "Sounds like the perfect time to me."

"Hurry," I panted as he slid his cock inside me. I wasn't worried about how long we'd take; I just wanted to feel him move inside me and make me come. Gripping his shoulders and wrapping my legs around his hips, I held on tight while he pounded into me.

"You're more gorgeous today than you were when I found you sleeping in your bed when I came to take you." He swiveled his hips, his cock dragging over my G-spot and making me clench around his hard length. "You were so damn hot that I knew I was fucked before you even opened your eyes."

"And look at us now."

His gaze dropped down, and he leaned back a little to watch his cock slide in and out of my body. "Come for me, baby. I wanna see your pussy squeeze me until I blow."

I slid my hand between us and flicked at my clit, making a growl creep up his chest. Each glide of his cock brought me closer to the edge, until I was suddenly flying over it and taking him with me. I slumped back against the mirror, panting for breath as he pulled out and cleaned me off with a washcloth.

"Hurry up, baby." He bent down to give me a kiss. Then he picked me up and set me on my feet, tucking himself back in and zipping up his pants. "We'd better get down there before hell freezes over and the Hounds of Hellfire President steps foot on Silver Saints soil."

I would have laughed, except it really did feel like hell was about to freeze over. I hurriedly changed my clothes while he lifted Molly out of the basinet we kept beside our bed. Her nursery was only one door down, but neither of us were ready for her to sleep in another room yet. I had no idea how he'd managed to have what was basically an entire house added to the back of the clubhouse in less than nine months, and I didn't really care. I was too busy being grateful that it was ready in time for me to decorate the nursery before I gave birth, even though we mostly used it like a big closet for Molly's stuff for now.

"It'll be okay," I reassured him as I smiled at the picture my tough biker made with our tiny baby girl in his arms. "Molly will melt all the ice, just like she does your heart."

Also by Fiona Davenport

Risqué Contracts Series
Penalty Clause
Contingency Plan
Fraternization Rule

Standalones
My Father's Best Friend
My Step-Dad's Brother
Not-So Temporarily Married
The One I Want for Christmas
The Virgin's Guardian

Yeah, Baby Series
Baby, You're Mine
Baby Steps
Baby, Don't Go
Dance With Me, Baby
I'm Yours, Baby

Brief Me, Baby

Play With Me, Baby

Safe With Me, Baby

Devour Me, Baby

Mafia Ties: Nic & Anna

Deception

Danger

Devotion

Mafia Ties: Brandon & Carly

Pursuit

Power

Passion

Mafia Ties: Christian & Mia

Obsession

Passion & Vows

Until Death Do We Part

For You, I Will

From This Day Forward

About the Author

The writing duo of Elle Christensen and Rochelle Paige team up under the Fiona Davenport pen name to bring you sexy, insta-love stories filled with alpha males. If you want a quick & dirty read with a guaranteed happily ever after, then give Fiona Davenport a try!

For all the STEAMY news about Fiona's upcoming releases... sign up for the mailing list!

Connect with us online:
www.fionadavenport.com

Printed in Great Britain
by Amazon